RAIN

GET A
CLUE!

D1111100

Library of Congress Control Number: 2022940759
ISBN 978-0-06-325613-2

23 24 25 26 27 PC/WOR 10 9 8 7 6 5 4 3 2 1

First Edition

RAINBOW HIGH™

GET A CLUE!

©MGA

Adapted by Steve Foxe

Based on the episodes written
by Elise Allen and Alex Mack

HARPER
An Imprint of HarperCollinsPublishers

AIDAN RUSSELL

AINSLEY SLATER

AVERY STYLES

BELLA PARKER

JADE HUNTER

POPPY ROWAN

RUBY ANDERSON

SKYLER BRADSHAW

SUNNY MADISON

VIOLET WILLOW

MS. LOU WRIGHT

©MGA

CHAPTER 1

"Hi-hi from Vi-Vi! My followers know what's up!"

Violet Willow—Vi-Vi to her fans— swung her selfie stick around, making sure her live-stream got a good look at the multicolored lockers lining the walls.

It was a *big* day for Violet, and she was dressed to impress in

head-to-toe purple.

"We're stepping in for day one at Rainbow High, the number one visual-arts high school *anywhere*!" Violet narrated to her streaming followers.

Violet was used to sharing her life with her fans. And her best friend, Sunny, following behind her, loved being Vi's most frequent guest star. They totally just *clicked* that way.

"So who's ready to—"

Violet stopped mid-sentence. Three of the *coolest* kids she had ever seen had just turned the corner, their outfits perfectly styled.

"Do they ... go here?" she whispered.

The flawless trio strutted toward Violet. She couldn't take her eyes off of them.

"Are you staring at us?" the girl in the center asked, her hair glittering in the light.

"N-no!" Violet stuttered, tucking her own purple hair behind her ears.

"Maybe a little," Sunny admitted, despite her BFF's bluff.

Violet took a deep breath. This was the biggest day of her life, and she wanted to make a good impression on these new (supercool) classmates.

"I'm Violet Willow," she said, extending her hand. "I'm filming my online reality show, *The Vi Life*. I'm sure you've heard of it. I have five hundred thousand followers across all of my social media accounts."

The only boy in the trio gave Violet a confused look.

"Uh . . . no," he replied. "And you can't take videos here without permission."

Violet wouldn't let his harsh response get her down. She reached into her bag and pulled out a clipboard.

"Permission forms—here you go!"

As the cool kids signed Violet's forms, Sunny stepped out from behind Violet to properly introduce herself.

"Hi! I'm Sunny Madison, Violet's BFF from forever," she said, her smile beaming as brightly as her yellow hair.

"Can you believe we *both* got into Rainbow High? We're, like,

twinsies!" Sunny said, squeezing Violet's shoulders.

"Not *exactly* twinsies," Violet quickly added, shuffling away. "I'm digital media focus, and Sunny's computer animation."

Every student at Rainbow High specializes in a particular type of art—and every student is *very* good at what they do. That's what makes the school so elite. If you're not setting the trends, someone else is going to snatch your spot before you know it.

"Wait, I know those names," the cool girl with chromatic eyeshadow said. "We're your prefects—the upper-classmen in charge of your floor."

The prefects struck a fierce pose.

"I'm Avery," the girl with the glittery hair said. "This is Ainsley and that's Aidan," she added, pointing first to the other girl and then to the boy. "But everyone calls us . . . the A's."

Before Violet or Sunny could respond, Avery pointed at a nearby stairway.

"Your rooms are two flights up. *Later.*"

And with that, the A's turned and left as quickly as they had shown up.

CHAPTER 2

"Whoa, hashtag Rainbow High goals!" Violet squealed. She was *beyond* impressed. The A's were everything she wanted to be!

As she tucked their signed permission slips into her bag, Violet was totally lost in thought, imagining herself becoming one of the

school's *coolest* students.

"Hey, earth to Violet!" Sunny said, waving her hand in her distracted BFF's face. Sunny pulled Violet toward the stairs. "You heard them—our dorms are this way. Let's go check them out!"

"What do you think the dorm room is like?" Sunny asked, skipping along the upstairs hallway with excitement. "It'll be so fun living *together* and not down the street!"

Before Violet could reply, Sunny came to a stop in front of a door.

"I found our names!" she squealed.

"Actually, wait . . ."

"Poppy Rowan, Sunny Madison, Skyler Bradshaw—okay, these girls all sound *so* cool," Sunny said, before turning to Violet with a frown. "But no Violet Willow. I don't get it. We both requested the same room, didn't we?"

Violet looked away.

"My, uh . . . mom must have for-gotten to send in the request form," Violet said, making up an excuse.

"But your mom is so on top of *everything*," Sunny replied. "I can't believe she'd forget something so important."

"Yeah, she, uh ... must have really dropped the ball," Violet said, avoiding her friend's eyes.

Just then, Violet pointed across the hall from Sunny's room. "Oh, look, I'm just over there!" she said, instantly cheering up as she spotted her name on a different door.

Violet skipped over to her own room and pointed to the names on the door, which absolutely did *not* include Sunny Madison.

"Not getting the same room is totally the *worst*," Violet said, "but now we can make more friends for us *both*! And that'll, like, totally be the best!"

Sunny looked heartbroken.

"Yeah, the best...." she replied.

Sunny was *really* looking forward to rooming with Violet. They had been best friends for most of

their lives, and rooming together was their chance to hang out *all* the time.

Living across the hall from each other would be cool, but not *as* cool.

"*So* sorry," Violet said, rushing into her new room. "Let's unpack and catch up later!"

Violet felt guilty for bending the truth with Sunny, but she wanted to meet everyone she possibly could, especially at a school like Rainbow High.

And as soon as Violet entered her own dorm room, she got her wish when she came face-to-face—

literally—with a girl wearing a lime-green beanie and some of the most *intense* makeup Violet had ever seen.

CHAPTER 3

"What's the matter—scared to meet your roommates?" the girl in green asked.

Violet jumped back. The girl laughed and high-fived two other girls behind her.

"Jade's makeup is *scary* good," a girl with fiery red hair and fresh street style said.

"I'm Ruby, and this is Bella," she added, pointing to the third girl, who wore pink. "Looks like we're your roommates!"

Before Violet could introduce herself, Bella realized why the new girl looked so familiar.

"Hold up! I recognize you—you're Violet Willow!" Bella said, eyes wide. "My social feed *lives* for you!"

Violet smiled and tossed her hair. She was used to being recognized, but it was an even better feeling to be recognized by her new peers at Rainbow High.

"That's me!" she said, passing

out permission forms. "And if you sign these releases, I'll be sure to introduce each of you to *all* my followers!"

Ruby grinned and tossed Violet a shoe.

"Sure thing—but first, hold this," she said, pulling out her phone to snap a picture. "I've got to get some of your influencer street cred!"

Violet struck a cute pose with the shoe, which had stunning art hand-drawn all over it.

"You painted this?" Violet asked Ruby.

"Custom kicks," Ruby replied. "It's

what I do. Well, one of the *many* things I do."

The girls took turns sharing why they were at Rainbow High. Ruby Anderson focused on visual art, whether that meant spicing up shoes, painting murals, or design-ing logos.

Violet immediately started fol-lowing her online to make sure she'd never miss a post. In fact, she was already dreaming up possible collaborations—maybe Ruby could design a new logo for *The Vi Life*!

Bella Parker, meanwhile, was studying set design. She had dreams of ending up on Broadway, creating the sets for smash-hit musicals.

If Bella *did* start working on Broadway, Violet could get backstage passes, interview the stars, and come up with some truly one-of-a-kind content.

And Violet already got a taste of Jade's skills. Jade Hunter was a *sick* makeup artist and could turn any face into a work of art. Violet *needed* to get Jade on her channel for a makeover video ASAP.

"Now that we're all here, we need to take a first-day selfie," Bella said. The girls leaned in close.

"Everyone say 'Own it,'" Ruby said, snapping the photo with Bella's phone.

"Own it!" they all shouted in unison.

"Totes on my Rainbow High day-one checklist," Bella said, showing her roommates the photo.

Violet could tell she was going to like these girls.

CHAPTER 4

Out in the hallway, Sunny followed *her* new roommates Skyler and Poppy to first-year orientation. As Skyler hurried them along, Sunny's phone buzzed.

"Ooh!" she said, checking the notification. "Remember how I told you about my best friend, Violet? She *just* posted a new pic."

Skyler and Poppy looked over Sunny's shoulder at the photo, which showed Violet smiling with Bella, Ruby, and Jade. Sunny couldn't help but frown. She and Violet had been besties *forever,* but now Sunny felt . . . left out.

Sunny was worried that she and her BFF might go down different paths at Rainbow High, especially now that they had different friends.

Skyler put her hand on Sunny's shoulder, snapping Sunny out of her funk. "Hey, Violet can still be your best friend even if she meets new people!" Skyler said.

"Besides, you get to meet new friends, too—like Skyler and me!" Poppy added. She pulled out her own phone and cued up a fast-paced dance song.

"I know what'll make it better," Poppy said, bouncing along to the music. "I dare you to be sad when you listen to *this*."

Skyler's reassurance and Poppy's hype beats cheered Sunny right up. Vi's roommates *did* look cool and fun, but Sunny's roommates were *just* as awesome.

And it's not like there's a limit on friends. In fact, Sunny couldn't wait to meet Violet's new pals and introduce Vi to Skyler and Poppy.

Skyler was at Rainbow High to become the next great fashion designer—one of the most competitive programs at the school. Her bright blue outfit showed off her

cutting-edge sense of style.

She could be shy about show-ing off her designs, but whenever she let someone get a peek at her sketches, it was *totally* obvious why she got accepted to the school. It was only a matter of time before

Skyler's designs were strutting down the hottest high-fashion catwalks in New York, Paris, London, Milan, and Tokyo.

Poppy, meanwhile, wanted to learn everything there was to know about music production. She was practically born with rhythm, and she had been making her own music since she was old enough to bang on pots and pans.

Now her preferred "instrument" was her computer, though, which she used to engineer *sick* beats. Her orange hair always stood out from the DJ booth.

Sunny was sure Violet would like these girls just as much as she did. Rainbow High was *full* of cool, talented, creative personalities.

Poppy, Sunny, and Skyler danced right into the orientation room, where they joined Bella, Ruby, Jade, and Violet.

"Ah, Vi!" Sunny shouted, reuniting with her BFF. It had only been a few minutes since they had seen each other, but they both had a *lot* of emotions in the meantime.

"Sunny, I'm sorry I rushed off so fast earlier," Violet said.

"Don't sweat it, bestie," Sunny

replied. "I'm bummed about the room situation, but I'm excited to meet more friends—for the two of us to share, just like you said."

Violet and Sunny gave each other a hug. The vibe was definitely still a *little* off, but they were working through it, just like besties are supposed to do. And as soon as their hug was over, Sunny pulled Skyler and Poppy over to meet Vi.

"I can't wait to introduce you to—" Sunny began, but she suddenly stopped talking when she looked up.

The girls wanted to show off and

get to know each other, but they immediately snapped to attention when an unsmiling woman in pointed glasses stepped to the front of the room.

CHAPTER 5

"I'm Lou Wright, the head of the school," the woman said. "Welcome to Rainbow High, where you will learn the tenets of grit, love, action, and moxie. I've put you in your runway group, the team that will *make or break you* this year."

All of the girls felt nervous. Ms. Wright had a reputation for taking

her role *very* seriously.

"Everyone look to your left, then look to your right," Ms. Wright commanded. "Not all of you will make it to the end of the year."

Violet gulped. Sunny had to focus to keep her knees from shaking.

"For your final project this semester, you will produce a complete runway show, including seven looks, hair, makeup, a set, and original music," Ms. Wright continued.

Ms. Wright looked each and every girl directly in the eyes.

"You will stage the show in front

of the entire school. Fail the runway show . . ."

Ms. Wright paused, letting the word "fail" hang in the air.

". . . and you can kiss Rainbow High goodbye."

As the girls stood quivering in their designer shoes, Ms. Wright turned and walked toward the door.

"Make no mistake—the semester will pass quickly," she said. "But you will have other assignments before the runway show."

"Take every opportunity you get at Rainbow High seriously,"

Ms. Wright warned. "Your first test is about to begin. Your advisor will explain more."

And with that, Ms. Wright strode out of the room, not even giving the girls a chance to ask any questions.

At first, everyone was too stunned

to speak. Then Jade finally gath-
ered the nerve to ask the question
everyone else was thinking.

"So ... where's our advisor?"

No one had any clue. They hadn't
received any directions or welcome
packets telling them more.

"Is this a test?" Bella asked nervously. "Are we already being tested?!"

"Good morning!" a voice said through a speaker in the ceiling. The girls all jumped. Rainbow High was *full* of surprises.

CHAPTER 6

"I'm Ms. Morton, your advisor," the voice on the speaker explained. "I'm sorry I can't be there in person, but when New York Fashion Week calls, you answer."

The intercom crackled a bit, but the girls could tell Ms. Morton was pure style and class just from her voice.

Jade turned to Bella and exchanged a fist bump. How cool was it that their advisor was off at New York Fashion Week?

"Rainbow High is tough, but it'll be easier if you can rely on one another," Ms. Morton continued.

"So welcome to your first assignment: the Glam Slam! It's a

scavenger hunt designed to help you get to know each other better. It's something of a school tradition— but don't think that means it will be easy!"

All of the girls' phones dinged at the same time.

Poppy held hers up to the group. On her screen was a rainbow-colored hourglass timer, already ticking away.

"You have until the sand runs out to complete

the scavenger hunt," Ms. Morton explained.

"Good luck—and take this seriously," Ms. Morton warned. "I'm sure Ms. Wright told you what happens when you don't succeed at Rainbow High."

The crackle of the overhead speaker went quiet.

Bella exchanged nervous glances with her runway group.

"She *cannot* mean we'll get cut if we fail a scavenger hunt," she said nervously. "It's only our first day!"

The other girls weren't so sure. Even through the static of the overhead speaker, Ms. Morton had seemed very serious. And Ms. Wright had made it pretty clear that Rainbow High accepted nothing less than perfection.

"She *totally* could mean it," Poppy said, watching the digital sand drop through the hourglass.

"Then where are the clues?" Violet said, rushing around the room, looking in every desk and under every object she could lift. "I *need* to be here—we need to get an A-plus on this scavenger hunt!"

"I think it's more of a pass-or-fail thing. . . ." Jade replied.

"You're not helping!" Violet hissed back. She looked at her phone—how was time already ticking away when they didn't even know where to start? This was *the* most embarrassing way to fail.

As the girls worried to themselves about the possibility of getting kicked out on day one, Skyler's phone lit up. She was so surprised, she almost dropped it.

"I got a clue!" Skyler gasped. "It says, 'Find the locker with Ruby's top-selling item on it.'"

"You sell things?" Skyler asked Ruby. "What do you sell? Jewelry,

designer handbags, sock pup-
pets?!" Just like Violet, Skyler was
already losing her cool. The threat
of failing the first assignment was
getting to the girls.

Before Ruby could explain,
though, Bella spoke up. Poppy,
Sunny, and Skyler didn't know
Violet's roommates too well just

yet, but Bella sure did.

"I know! Ruby showed us in the room!" Bella exclaimed.

"She sells clothes she customizes with paint, and they're, like, *super* fashionable and cool. I'd totally wear them. Anyway, her top seller is . . . sneakers!"

"You got it, B," Ruby said, snapping her fingers. "And thanks for the hype. Now, let's go to the lockers and find the next clue!"

The hunt was on—and the girls' future at Rainbow High was on the line!

CHAPTER 7

The girls spread out, scanning the lockers on every floor. Time was running out *way* faster than they expected. They absolutely could *not* fail their first assignment.

Poppy kept her eyes glued to the rainbow-colored metal lockers,

desperate for a clue.

"Sneakers, sneakers . . . Score!"
she shouted.

Poppy snatched a Polaroid

picture of Ruby's custom shoes from the bottom of a locker door.

"Sweet kicks," she said, admiring the shoes. Then she turned the

photo over. "And a clue on the back!"

The other girls rushed to her side as she read it out loud.

"'The locker combination is the number of awards Bella won for set design in middle school, at Cinched Drama Fest, and at Runway Riot,'" Poppy said. "Wow, sounds like you're a big deal in set design."

"Seriously." Jade smirked. "Over-achieving much?"

"It's my passion," Bella replied. She blushed and tucked her hair behind her ears. "I put a lot of myself into it, so I win . . . a lot of awards."

Violet didn't want to waste another second. She waved her arms at the sky.

"How many?" she asked hysterically. "We need cold, hard numbers!"

Bella counted on her fingers. "Oh! Eight in middle school, then five . . . and thirteen!"

Skyler immediately started typing

the code into the locker.

With a pop, the locker sprang open. Inside was a rainbow-covered hair iron with a clue attached to it.

Skyler read the clue to the other girls. "'Go where you'd find this hair iron, then look for something Violet sponsors.'" Skyler shot Violet a confused look. "Violet, what do you sponsor?"

Sunny jumped right in to answer. "She sponsors a ton of amazing products. Absolutely every brand wants the *Vi Life* stamp of approval."

Sunny couldn't stop singing her BFF's praises.

"Her photography won so many awards, she got a bunch of followers, and now she's a *major* influencer.

And the videos she posts? The best!"

Violet clutched her hands to her chest. "You really mean that?" she asked.

"We get it—Sunny's super supportive," Jade said, rolling her eyes. "Let's take these good vibes to the salon, because that's where our next clue is!"

Sunny and Violet gave each other a quick hug, and then the girls took Jade's advice. They rushed down the hallway, following the signs to the salon.

"This would be easier if we knew where all the rooms were,"

Poppy said.

"I think this is what they call learning under pressure," Ruby replied.

In the salon room, the girls scoured every nook and cranny for any sign of a clue. Poppy, though, was scrolling through her phone instead.

"Stalking your social media now, Vi," she said. "Wait, this must be it—hair foam! It's the only product you sponsor that can be found in a salon."

A can of that same hair foam was right in front of Skyler. She grabbed

it and turned it in every direction, but there was no clue.

"Hold up," Ruby said. She took the can from Skyler and pressed down on the nozzle. A rolled-up piece of paper popped out!

"'One of you published cartoons

in a magazine,'" Ruby said, reading the clue. "'Find the cover of that magazine and get your next clue.'"

This time it was Violet's turn to hype up her friend.

"It's Sunny!" she practically screamed. "It was published on the last day of sixth grade, and I was so, *so* proud of her."

"My mom took us for makeovers to celebrate. Hashtag middle school goals!"

"I remember that," Sunny added. "It was my first gel mani-pedi!" She smiled ear to ear hearing her BFF remember that special day.

Maybe she and Vi would be okay after all.

"Amazing story, loved it, might even journal about it," Jade cut in sarcastically. "*Which magazine was it?!*"

"Oh, right!" Sunny said, remembering the scavenger hunt. "*Winnerz.* And I know where we can find the cover! Follow me!"

CHAPTER 8

The girls followed Sunny through the hall to a framed cover of *Winnerz*.

"Ta-da!" she said, pointing to the cover. "But I don't see a note. Frowny face."

"Never surrender!" Bella said, reaching behind the frame. She turned her arm this way and that,

searching for something. . . .

Just as Bella suspected—a hidden clue tucked behind the frame!

"Your next clue is on the exact fabric Skyler used to make the dress *Sizzle* called 'the top summer outfit inspo of the year,'" Bella read out loud. All eyes turned to Skyler.

"For reals?!" Violet asked, clearly impressed.

"Legendary!" Poppy added.

Skyler blushed and looked away. She wasn't used to this kind of attention. She liked her clothes to speak for themselves.

"I didn't submit it or anything," she said quietly. "*Sizzle* just found the dress and wrote that."

"Um, that's even cooler," Bella said, giving Skyler a hip bump and a wink. "That means your work speaks for itself. Own it—I would. And I bet we'll find the fabric in the runway classroom!"

With time slipping through their fingers, Skyler led the girls to the fashion studio.

Skyler had scoped the studio out as soon as she got to the school, so she knew exactly where to go—but not where to find the clue once she got there.

She scratched her chin and looked around the walls at the different fabrics.

There were velvets, faux furs, and cotton fabrics in every color the girls could imagine. Not to mention state-of-the-art sewing machines and printers designed to print any design imaginable.

"That's it," Skyler shouted, spotting a jacket covered in glittering rainbow sequins. "That's the fabric I used for the dress!"

"Whoa, that's so chic," Violet said. "No wonder you won that award."

As Skyler blushed at the compliment, Poppy reached into the jacket's chest pocket and found the next clue!

"Jammin'!" Poppy exclaimed. "This one's about me! 'What satellite radio station heard Poppy's music and let her guest DJ?'" Poppy knew the answer right away. "That's an easy one—station 103! Give me enough time, though, and you'll hear me on way more channels."

"I totally believe in you, but what does '103' mean as a clue?" Sunny asked, looking anxiously at the

digital hourglass. "Is the next clue playing on the radio? Someone tune in and find out!"

Poppy switched her phone's radio to 103, and an upbeat song started playing. The girls couldn't help but bounce along. If this scavenger hunt wasn't such a race against the clock, they'd have *way* more time to party.

But partying would have to wait—they *still* didn't have the next clue.

"I never thought I'd say this," Poppy admitted, turning the volume down on the music. "But now is *not* the time for a dance party. If the clue isn't on the radio, does anyone else have any ideas?"

The girls' brief distraction from the scavenger hunt snapped them back to reality. Bella bit at her nails and searched her thoughts. She could *not* flunk out so fast.

Her future as an award-winning set designer relied on her succeeding at Rainbow High.

"The sand's almost out!" Bella showed her phone to the other girls. They had found and solved clues relating to every girl except Jade, and now their time was almost gone.

"This has to be about Jade," Bella shouted. "Everyone think!"

"Uh, maybe 103 is the temperature that Jade's makeup melts at?" Violet offered.

"Or the number of palettes in her collections?" Ruby suggested.

"Maybe it's how many brushes she uses when she gives makeovers?" Sunny added.

"No, no, and not even close," Jade said.

If they couldn't figure out what "103" meant—and soon—their first day at Rainbow High . . . might be their last!

CHAPTER 9

"Can't get cut, can't get cut," Skyler repeated nervously. She closed her eyes tight and thought about the "103" clue.

"I've got it!" she shouted, already heading for the door. "The number 103 must be a *classroom*. It's so obvious. Hurry, we don't have any time to waste!"

Six of the girls rushed into the hall, but Poppy was still jamming to station 103's beats. "Come on, Poppy!" Jade growled, pulling the orange-clad DJ with her.

"This is how I celebrate!" Poppy protested, finally turning the music all the way off.

Skyler and the others didn't make it too far, though. As soon as Jade and Poppy caught up to them in the hallway, they saw that their path was being blocked ... by the A's!

"Hi there. Please excuse us," Jade said, trying to brush past the older kids.

Violet pulled Jade aside and whispered to her.

"Um, Jade—these are the A's."

"The who?" Jade responded.

"Our prefects. They run our floor," Violet said, turning back to smile at Ainsley, Avery, and Aidan.

"Well, our prefects are going to cause us to flunk out of this school if they don't let us by," Jade whisper-shouted back.

"Wait, are you doing Ms. Morton's

Glam Slam?" Avery asked, stepping out of formation with the other A's.

Bella held up her phone, showing Avery how little time was left on the hourglass. Her hand was trembling so much, it took Avery a moment to realize what she was looking at.

"We're almost done with it, but we have, like, no time left to spare!" Bella managed to squeak out.

Avery stepped to the side, and Aidan and Ainsley followed.

"Good luck, girls," she said, tossing her stunning hair behind her. "The Glam Slam is a rite of passage for new Rainbow High students. It's stressful, but try to enjoy it."

"Ah, they're just like us!" Violet whispered to Sunny.

When the girls finally reached room 103, Skyler skidded to a stop, the rubber of her sneakers

squeaking against the floor. Tucked right into the room number was an envelope. It had to be the next—and hopefully final—clue!

"'One of you has your own makeup line,'" Skyler read. "'What's it called?'"

"It's got to be you, right?" Ruby asked Jade. After all, Jade's makeup was *scary good*. All the girls knew how to paint their faces, but Jade's skill was next-level.

Besides, she was the only member of the runway group left without a clue!

"I'm still tweaking it, but it's

going to be *sick*," Jade answered. "It's called Look Up, because that's what I have to tell people a *zillion* times when I'm doing their eye makeup."

"Look up?" Bella repeated. All at once, the girls craned their necks to look toward the ceiling. Above them, way too high for any of them to reach, was a poster—the final clue!

Bella got pumped up.

"Okay, we can do this," she roared. "Human ladder! Everyone on each other's shoulders!"

Bella bent down and wove her hands together. Ruby raised one foot to start climbing. If this was what it took to stay enrolled at Rainbow High, she was ready.

"Wait!" Skyler said, stopping Ruby before she and Bella could start their human ladder. "I've seen that poster before. It was on the wall in the classroom where we started!"

eyes turned to room 101, right across the hall. But then Sunny looked down at her phone. There were only a few drops of digital sand left in the hourglass.

"We've gotta go!" she exclaimed. They had come too far to fail the scavenger hunt now, so close to the finish line!

CHAPTER 10

"The poster!" Skyler said, pointing to a matching one inside room 101.

As soon as the girls entered the doorway, lights of every color started flashing all around them.

"We did it!" Violet shouted. "Wait, we *did* do it, right? These aren't failure lights to tell us we've been expelled?"

The speaker in the ceiling crackled to life again.

"Congratulations, you've won the Glam Slam!" Ms. Morton said, tuning in remotely from New York Fashion Week. "And now you have a group of friends you can count on for everything Rainbow High throws at you."

Bella, Ruby, Poppy, Sunny, Jade, Skyler, and Violet looked at each other. The scavenger hunt had been, like, *totally* stressful, but they actually had learned a lot about each other in the process.

"And that's not all," Ms. Morton continued. "Check out the desk.

Special gifts for each of your special talents."

The girls rushed right over to the desk. It was covered in art supplies, fabric, makeup brushes, and even a new sewing machine, camera, and DJ equipment! Rainbow High spared no expenses.

Violet, Sunny, and the others could barely believe their eyes. Each girl picked up the supplies and showed them off to their new friends.

"Wow!"

"No way!"

"Major!"

"This is, like, totally state of the art."

The sounds of excitement bounced around the room. All that talk about Rainbow High being the best school around? It wasn't just talk.

"This is sick!" Jade added— practically her trademark phrase.

"But Ms. Morton, when do we get to meet you?"

"Soon, once my work here at Fashion Week is done," the speaker replied. "You girls can clearly manage yourselves. To an extent, anyway. Although I'll certainly pop back in to help you as needed. After all, your big runway project will be here before you know it."

The girls all looked at each other. Ms. Morton wasn't going to let them forget *that* little detail.

"In the meantime, enjoy." Then the speaker went silent once again.

Violet had known that Rainbow

High would be *intense*, but she didn't realize it would be *this* wild. When she and Sunny first walked through the doors just hours earlier, they couldn't have known that their first assignment would send them racing all over the school—quite the orientation activity!

And while their friendship felt rocky for a second there, the Glam Slam reminded both Violet and Sunny that BFFs really can mean "forever."

But the highlight of the day wasn't the scavenger hunt or even all of the supplies Ms. Morton surprised the girls with at the end.

For Bella, Ruby, Poppy, Sunny, Jade, Skyler, and Violet, the best part of their first day at Rainbow High was meeting each other! No matter how tough the assignments ahead might be—especially that runway project looming over the rest of the semester—they would tackle them together!